# IN THE DOGHOUSE

By Lisa Banim
Based on the series
created by Terri Minsky

Watch it on

DISNEY CHANNEL

abc kids

DISNEY PRESS

VOLO

New York

Printed in the United States of America

First Edition
1 3 5 7 9 10 8 6 4 2

Library of Congress Catalog Card Number on file.

ISBN 0-7868-4637-2
For more Disney Press fun, visit www.disneybooks.com
Visit DisneyChannel.com

CHAPTER

1

"Quit channel surfing," Lizzie McGuire told her best friend, David "Gordo" Gordon. "You're making me dizzy!"

"Sure, whatever," said Gordo. But his eyes remained glued to the McGuires' TV screen, and the channels continued to change.

With a sigh, Miranda Sanchez reached over and snatched the remote from Gordo's hand. "Enough already," she said. "We're going to pick one show and stick with it."

"Who watches the tube like that?" Gordo

complained. "At least let me surf through the commercials." He grabbed the remote back.

"Whoa, wait a sec!" Miranda cried as a huge, white, luxury ship sailed onto the TV screen. "There's the ad for that cruise Kate's taking with her mom next week—the *Bermuda Queen*."

"Change the channel, please," said Lizzie with a sigh. "You're making me seasick."

"Life is so unfair," Miranda complained. "Why does Kate Sanders, Queen of Mean, get to go on a fabulous trip during spring break?"

"While *we* go on exotic trips to the video store and the Hillridge Mall," Lizzie added.

it's scary, but i think i see a brand-new TV show being launched right in front of me. it's called *The Longest, Most Boring Spring Break Ever!* Unfortunately, i'm the star.

"Come on, guys," Gordo said. "It won't be that bad. It's a week off to do whatever we want!"

"Like what?" Miranda asked.

"Like maybe we could even take Vice Principal Putney's Civic Challenge and try to win the Hillridge Community Helper Award," suggested Gordo.

Miranda rolled her eyes. "Oh puh-leeze. That guy has got to lighten up already. What was with that gung-ho speech he gave at the special assembly today?"

"I believe it had something to do with making spring break *worthwhile* for a change," said Gordo in his straight-A-plus student voice. "You know, instead of lying around, playing video games, and hanging at the mall."

"He's on a real crusade, all right," Lizzie said. She lowered her voice to impersonate the super-strict vice principal. "Leading a special, extracurricular mission for the creation of 'civic-minded' young people."

How about a special, extra-curricular mission for the creation of the perfect spring break? Okay, it should come with tropical smoothies, no annoying little brother, amazing beachwear accessories, and an ocean view that'll knock my flip-flops off!

"You're forgetting one very important detail," Gordo pointed out. "Vice Principal Putney and our newly elected mayor are old buddies. And Mayor Robertson really likes this 'good citizen' idea."

Lizzie sighed. "And, aren't there some sort of *prizes* involved?"

"Yeah," said Gordo. "The mayor's office will be giving one thousand dollars to the student who wins the Hillridge Community Helper Award. Plus, you get a certificate and a dinner for your family at the mayor's mansion."

"One thousand dollars is seriously nothing to sneeze at," Lizzie admitted.

"Chump change it's not," agreed Gordo.

"And I guess dinner with the mayor would be kind of cool," added Lizzie. "My mom and dad would be seriously psyched if I won something like that."

Miranda shuddered. "Count me out," she said. "In *my* opinion, no amount of money or glory is worth all that work over vacation." She frowned at the TV. "There's that cruise ad again! Aargh!"

"Actually, Miranda, a Community Helper Award would be a very good thing to have on your school record," Gordo pointed out. "And the winner is sure to get his or her picture on the front page of the *Hillridge Daily News*."

"You know, you may have a point there, Gordo," Lizzie said, tapping her chin with her fingers. "It would be nice to do something for the community. And getting an award on our school records wouldn't hurt, either."

"Not to mention one thousand buckaroos to spend at the mall," Miranda grudgingly added. "*If* we were going to spend spring break working for a worthy cause. Which we *aren't*."

"Hmmm," said Lizzie. "*What* could we do to help the community?"

"No, Lizzie," Miranda warned. "Be strong."

"Maybe we could come up with a way to make the recycling center more efficient," Gordo said, sitting up straighter on the couch. "Or do a traffic-flow study on Main Street. We need something that will blow Larry Tudgeman out of the water for sure."

Lizzie rolled her eyes. Gordo has yet to get over losing the Science Olympics to the Tudge, she thought.

"Gordo," Miranda said as she flipped channels. "You are really scaring me now. And— omigosh, there's that cruise ad *again*! How many times do they have to torture us with the *Bermuda Queen* of Mean?" Glaring, she pointed the remote at the TV and changed the channel one more time.

Instantly, a basket of cute little puppies appeared on the screen. A lady on the local news was telling viewers that these puppies were being housed at the Hillridge Animal Shelter, but they were currently up for adoption.

"Oooh!" Lizzie said. "Have you ever seen anything so *adorable*?"

"Gee, thanks, Lizzie," Matt McGuire said, bounding into the room. "Funny, everyone always says that about me."

Ha! Why don't i dump my "adorable" little brother in a laundry basket with a sign that says "Free to Good Home in the Arctic Circle." Now *that's* what i'd call a truly valuable community service!

"Go away, pest," Lizzie told Matt, turning the volume higher. "We're trying to listen to the news here."

"Right," Matt said. "How stupid do you think I am? You *never* listen to the news."

"Unfortunately, the Hillridge Animal Shelter is completely full right now," said the lady on TV. "And we're running out of funds to create badly needed space."

"That's terrible," Miranda said. "Those poor little puppies!"

"You don't like dogs," Gordo reminded her.

Miranda looked indignant. "I like them," she said. "I'm just a tiny bit afraid of really big ones."

Lizzie giggled. "You mean like that 'really big' rat of a dog you thought was after you when we were investigating what happened to the missing Audrey Albright?"

"Hey, he *sounded* big," Miranda replied.

"So, remember, the Hillridge Animal Shelter badly needs your donations," the lady on TV continued. "Please help us help our animal friends."

"That's it!" Lizzie cried, jumping off the couch. "That's how we can help the community—by helping the Hillridge Animal Shelter!"

"Good idea," Miranda said. "How?"

"Well, maybe we could walk and dog-sit my neighbors' dogs during the day," she said, "and give the money we earn to the shelter."

"No scientific angle," Gordo said. "No heavy analysis using mathematical computations, either. *But* it sounds like a plan."

"Sounds like a lot of hard work," Miranda protested.

"Just think of all the poor, cute little animals we'd be helping," Lizzie pleaded. "And it'll be fun." She looked hopefully at her friends.

"Okay, I'm in," Gordo said.

Miranda frowned but finally nodded. "Me, too," she said with a shrug.

Matt snorted and flipped the channel to one

of his favorite shows, *Taking Care of Business: You and Your Money*.

"News bulletin folks," he said, "any business venture of Lizzie's is doomed to fail. . . . *However*, if you want my *expert* advice, I'd be happy to help. For a small fee, of course. Say, a ninety-five percent cut of the cash once Lizzie wins the Hillridge Community Helper Award."

"I don't think so, Dog Breath," Lizzie said.

Matt shrugged and turned his attention back to his show. "Suit yourself," he told her.

Listen up, Matt the Brat! i have a news bulletin for *you*. My dog-walking biz will be a *huge* success. i'll save the day at the shelter *and* be honored with the Community Helper Award. Just wait and see!

CHAPTER

2

The next morning, Lizzie hit the snooze button on her alarm clock three times. She'd been so excited about her new dog-walking business that she'd stayed up half the night designing flyers and posters on her computer.

"Snoozers are losers!" Matt called through the bedroom door. "Rule Numero Uno in the biz world."

Lizzie threw her purple tasseled pillow at the door. Hard. She hated to admit it, but Matt was right. It was time to get to work. She, Miranda, and Gordo were going to put up posters on the way to school. It was the last day before their weeklong spring break, so it was a great time to advertise their new business and start lining up customers for the week ahead.

Lizzie pulled her robe over her pajamas and trudged down the hall to the bathroom. She almost ran into Matt, who was already fully dressed and heading downstairs. "Last one to eat breakfast is an ugly freak!" he called over his shoulder.

Sometimes it's not even worth the energy to deal with spiky-headed little dorks. Especially ones to whom you are unfortunate enough to be related.

"Doggy Day Care," Mr. McGuire said. "That's a great name, honey."

Lizzie had just finished showing her parents

the posters and flyers she had printed out while she was getting ready for school. "Thanks," she said. "I like it, too."

Matt seemed to be choking on his cornflakes. "Are you sure about that?" he said. "A lame name is Business Mistake Numero Two."

Lizzie glared at him.

"Just a little expert advice," he said, grinning. "Absolutely free."

Mrs. McGuire looked over Lizzie's shoulder at one of the posters. "And that's a cute slogan, too, Lizzie," she said. "'You Can Trust Your Pup to Us.'" Then she frowned. "Um, honey," she said. "You did mean *pup*, didn't you?"

Lizzie looked back at the poster. "Oh no!" she cried. "How could this have happened?"

"What, honey?" Mr. McGuire asked, looking concerned. "What's the matter?"

Lizzie stared at the poster. It didn't say "Pup." It said "Pop." I must have been so tired I made a typo, she thought. Then she heard Matt snicker.

Quickly, Lizzie began to flip through the other posters. One of them said, "Doogy Day Care." Another said, "Boogy Day Care." And a third one read, "Doggy Who Cares?"

By now, Matt was laughing so hard he almost squirted juice out of his nose. "Did I happen to mention Business Rule Numero Three?" he asked.

There was no question about it. Matt had gone into her room while she'd been in the bathroom and sabotaged all of her posters! "Why you little—" Lizzie began, lunging across the table.

"Whoa, time out, you two!" Mrs. McGuire cried. "What's going on here?"

Lizzie's eyes filled with tears. "Matt wrecked my posters!" she said. "And I worked really hard on them."

Matt held up his hands. "I don't know what you're talking about," he protested. "I didn't touch your stupid posters."

"No, you touched my computer!" Lizzie cried.

Mrs. McGuire sighed. "Lizzie, you go on upstairs and fix the posters. I'll pack you a breakfast to go."

Matt jumped up from the table. "Gee, I think I hear the school bus," he said, grabbing his knapsack. "See you all later!"

"Just a minute, young man," Mr. McGuire said.

But Matt was already racing out the door.

"We'll deal with you later," his dad called after him.

Lizzie ran up to her bedroom and sat down at her computer. In ten seconds, she had figured out that the errors on the posters and flyers were no accident. Matt was guilty, and she knew it because the little creep had failed to cover his tracks.

Yes, the posters and flyers on her computer screen were now riddled with errors. But the night before, Lizzie had e-mailed *perfect* versions of them to Miranda and Gordo. When she checked her e-mail "sent" box, she saw that those versions were still perfect.

Sighing angrily, Lizzie printed out the perfect versions of the posters and flyers from her e-mail box and deleted the error-ridden "Matt" versions on her computer screen.

if only i could push a button and delete Matt that easily.

Finally, Lizzie was ready to go. She headed back downstairs with a new set of advertisements in her knapsack. "Bye, Mom. Bye, Dad," she called on her way out the door.

Mrs. McGuire came out of the kitchen with a brown paper bag. Mr. McGuire was right behind her. "Lizzie, don't forget your breakfast," her mom said. "I packed you an orange and a granola bar."

"Thanks," Lizzie said, taking the bag.

"Honey, there's just one more thing we wanted to talk to you about," said Mrs. McGuire.

Mr. McGuire cleared his throat. "I know we gave you permission last night to start this doogy—er, *doggy*—business," he said.

"Because it's for charity," Mrs. McGuire quickly added.

"But it's going to be a tough job, Lizzie," Mr. McGuire warned. "Do you think you'll be up to all the responsibilities?"

"Of course, Dad," Lizzie said. "Responsibility is my middle name, remember?"

Her parents exchanged glances. "Right," Mrs. McGuire said. "But keep in mind that those responsibilities include any doggy messes along the way. Got it?"

"Got it," Lizzie replied. Then she checked her wristwatch. She was already late for her meeting with Gordo and Miranda.

Waving to her parents, she bolted for the door. It was time to get Doggy Day Care off the ground!

* * *

On their way to school, Gordo and Miranda helped Lizzie distribute her Doggy Day Care flyers in mailboxes all over their neighborhood. They put up posters, too.

"We've put up a zillion of these," Miranda said, taping poster zillion and one to a tree. "I sure hope we get some customers."

"Don't count on it," snapped a nasty voice behind them. "Those posters are pitiful."

Lizzie whirled around. Kate Sanders and her pal Claire were standing there, smirking.

"It figures Lizzie and Miranda will be taking care of *dogs* over spring break," Kate said to Claire. "Takes one to know one, right?"

**Right, Kate. Which means you and Claire should be in the *witch*-sitting business. *Aargh!***

18

Miranda's eyes narrowed. "I hope you have a real good time over spring break, Kate," she said. "I hear those cruises can be a lot of fun. Like that great luxury liner . . . what was it called? Oh, yeah, *Titanic.*"

Kate looked furious. "For your information, I'm not going on that cruise anymore," she said. "My mom has a super-important business meeting in Paris, so she had to cancel the cruise."

"So, now you get to go to Paris instead?" said Miranda, incredulous. "What a *disappointment.*"

"Yeah, Paris. What a letdown," Gordo scoffed.

"Not that it's any of your business, but I've decided to stay here in Hillridge for the break," Kate said. "So, I'll be around to watch your little doggy enterprise *flop.*"

With a mean smile, she and Claire both flipped their hair and swept past Lizzie and her friends.

Gee, that went well.

# CHAPTER

## 3

At lunchtime, the vice principal marched into the Hillridge Junior High cafeteria.

"*Ay, carumba*," Miranda muttered. "It's the last day of school before break. What does the man want with us *now*?"

Mr. Putney was a giant man with a large square chin. He wore his hair in a military buzz cut, and whenever he spoke to kids in the halls, he sounded like a drill sergeant giving orders to troops.

Most of the kids at Hillridge were wary of the

man, so it was no surprise that when he clapped his hands and called for everyone to pay attention, the entire room got quiet in record time.

"Boys and girls," the vice principal announced, "I just want to tell you how pleased I am that some of you are stepping up to take on the Hillridge Junior Civic Challenge. I've already heard about some very interesting projects!"

"Great," Gordo whispered. "I'll bet you anything Larry Tudgeman is doing my traffic-flow pattern analysis."

"For example," Vice Principal Putney went on, "Lizzie McGuire. *Lizzie*, where are you?"

*Omigosh*, he said my name, realized Lizzie, and in front of the whole school! Her face reddened and she sank lower in her seat.

Um, Lizzie who? Nope, sorry. Never heard of her.

Miranda nudged Lizzie with her elbow. "Lizzie, raise your hand," she whispered.

Lizzie smiled weakly and waggled her fingers at Vice Principal Putney.

"Oh, there you are, Lizzie. Stand up so everyone can see you!" he boomed as he held up one of her flyers. "Ms. McGuire is starting a dog-walking business to benefit the Hillridge Animal Shelter."

Sheepishly, Lizzie stood up, dragging Gordo and Miranda with her. "My friends are helping, too," she declared. "We're a team, actually. Team Doggy Day Care."

Laughter at the funny name rolled through the cafeteria. But a lot of kids clapped, too.

"Thank you, Lizzie," Miranda muttered, "ever so much for this public humiliation."

"Sorry," Lizzie whispered. She, Miranda, and Gordo sat down again—*fast.*

Just then, Kate jumped to her feet from a table behind them. "Vice Principal Putney?" she called, giving him a big cheerleader wave. "I have a community service project, too!"

Vice Principal Putney beamed. "Wonderful!" he said. "And what is your project, Ms. Sanders?"

"Well . . ." Kate looked around the cafeteria and smiled, stalling for time. Lizzie could tell that she was trying to think fast. "My friends and I are going to run a fund-raising drive for the cheerleading squad, so we can finally buy new pom-poms. For a ten-buck donation, we'll use the yearbook design facilities to place anyone's photo over a picture of a Hillridge cheerleader uniform. Then all the photos will be displayed on our special 'Now even YOU can be a cheer-leader' booster board! How cool is that?"

It was pretty obvious that Kate expected the whole place to erupt with excitement, and her fellow cheerleaders did cheer enthusiastically. Some football players clapped halfheartedly, too. But most of the faces in the cafeteria just stared blankly at the cheer queen.

Congratulations, Kate, you've come up with a fund-raising idea that has all the appeal of liver-flavored ice cream.

"We'll have a table set up outside the yearbook office all afternoon so everyone can sign up between classes," Kate quickly added.

Gordo shook his head. "I don't think Kate gets the whole 'civic-minded' thing," he whispered to Lizzie and Miranda. "Cheerleading isn't part of the *larger* community. Just the *school* community. And a pretty small percentage of *that*."

Miranda shrugged. "What do you expect? She's *Kate*, remember? She thinks her own little world is the whole universe."

Vice Principal Putney cleared his throat. "Very . . . er, *interesting*, Ms. Sanders," he said.

Kate sneered triumphantly at Lizzie as she sat down. Then she turned to Claire and said, "With all the pathetic, loser, cheerleader wannabes in this school, we're sure to make a ton of money for the squad's new pom-poms."

Lizzie overheard the remark, and her mouth dropped open.

That is *so* incredibly nasty. Even for Kate.

Miranda caught Kate's mean remark, too. But she wasn't about to sit still for it.

"I don't get it," Miranda declared to Lizzie in a voice loud enough for kids at the tables around them to hear. "Why would anybody want to pay to be on a board with a bunch of *witches*?"

A kid sitting nearby couldn't help laughing. "Hey, that's a good one," he cried. "The witch board!"

Some kids around him giggled.

"*Which* board?" the kid continued. "The *witch* board!"

More kids giggled as the "witch board" joke was passed from one table to the next until the entire cafeteria was laughing.

Kate's eyes narrowed in fury. She leaned toward Lizzie's table and whispered, "Let me spell something out for you, doggy geeks. *My* brilliant idea is going to W-I-N the Community Helper Award. *Your* stupid little pooper-scooper business is going to F-A-I-L. And that's a promise."

"Bring it on," snapped Miranda.

Lizzie hated confrontations, but she had to back Miranda—and defend her own business.

"Yeah!" she said.

Clever comeback, McGuire. You're really in the zone today.

# CHAPTER

## 4

"Lizzie McGuire, please report to Vice Principal Putney's office," a voice commanded over the PA system in the middle of Lizzie's Spanish class. "On the double."

*Great,* Lizzie thought with a gulp. What did I do now? And how many days detention will it get me?

While Principal Tweedy ran the school and occasionally handled disciplinary issues, it was Vice Principal Putney who dealt with the most troublesome, delinquent kids. Lizzie had never been called to the vice principal's office before. She didn't even know any of the kids who had.

"*Adios*," Gordo told her. "I mean, good luck."

"It was nice knowing you," Miranda added.

Lizzie sighed. "Thanks a lot, guys." She nervously gathered up her books and dragged herself slowly toward the door.

i have a bad feeling about this. One of those i'm-going-to-end-up-in-detention-for-the-rest-of-my-life feelings.

But I haven't done anything wrong, Lizzie reminded herself. Not that I know of, anyway. And Vice Principal Putney seemed really impressed by my Doggy Day Care project.

So what's the deal? What's this all about? i demand answers!

As Lizzie headed down the hall toward the main office, she spotted Kate bossing around two geeky boys from the Audio-Visual Club. The thin, pale kids with thick, black-rimmed glasses were struggling to move a large table against a wall by the door.

"Over a little more to the left now," Kate commanded. "No, *left*. Hello? Do you know your left from your right? I said *left*, you morons!"

Lizzie shook her head in disgust. From what she'd seen between classes, it didn't look like Kate was getting many takers for her lame cheerleader "booster board" sign-up. Obviously, she was moving her table from its spot by the yearbook office to the school's front doors. It would be her last chance to snag some willing victims on their way out of school before the weeklong break.

Lizzie arrived at Vice Principal Putney's office and knocked on the door. "It's Lizzie McGuire, sir," she said nervously.

"Ms. McGuire!" the vice principal boomed. "Come in."

Lizzie walked into the room and nearly tripped over a large fur rug. "Woof!" the rug barked.

"Yikes!" Lizzie cried, jumping back in surprise. The "rug" was a huge, hairy golden retriever.

"Don't mind Baxter," Mr. Putney said. "He's very friendly. In fact, he's a champion show dog. His official name is Sergeant Putney Golden Baxter."

Lizzie smiled at the dog. "What a nice name," she said, sitting down in the visitor's chair. "Good doggy." The golden retriever barked once, then yawned and looked away.

"So, you're probably wondering why I asked you to come in," said the vice principal.

"Y-yes, sir," Lizzie stammered, trying not to stare at the man's large square chin, which seemed to take up most of his unsmiling face—beneath the buzz cut and the intense eyes.

"Tell me, Ms. McGuire, would you consider yourself a very *responsible* young person?" he asked, leaning forward across his desk.

Uh-oh, here it comes. The *responsibility* lecture. The price for doing the terrible thing i did, which was . . . Um, excuse me, sorry? *What* did i do exactly?

"Lizzie, I have a problem. I'm leaving town for a week over spring break. Unfortunately, my regular dog-sitter is on vacation, the local kennel is full, and I never, *ever* leave Baxter alone."

"Um, right," Lizzie said. "Of course not."

"Well," Vice Principal Putney went on, "my plane leaves at one o'clock on Saturday and my sister Prudence, who has already agreed to look after Baxter while I'm away, will be out of town until six o'clock that evening. Do you think you are responsible enough to take on the job of caring for Baxter for an entire afternoon?"

Yes, yes, yes! I'm not in the doghouse after all! And the vice principal is going to trust his champion pup to *me*, Super Community Helper Lizzie McGuire!

Lizzie almost fell off her chair in relief, but she was glad she didn't. She would have landed right on Baxter, and her first client had just hired her to *sit* his dog, not sit *on* it.

"No problem, sir," Lizzie answered. "Responsibility is my middle name." And Doggy Day Care is officially in business! she thought.

On the way home from school, Lizzie told Miranda and Gordo all about her meeting with Vice Principal Putney.

"So we have our very first client," Lizzie said happily. "How cool is that?"

"It would be a lot cooler if it wasn't *Vice Principal Putney's* dog," Miranda said. "What if something goes wrong? We'll be dog food. Extra-crunchy dog food."

"Nothing's going to go wrong, Miranda," Lizzie said. "I have everything all planned out."

"Uh, Lizzie?" Gordo said, frowning. "Do you notice anything different about this street?"

"No," Lizzie said. "It looks exactly the way it did this morning when we walked to school."

Gordo shook his head. "Look again," he said.

Lizzie gazed up and down the tree-lined street.

"My Doggy Day Care posters!" she cried. "They're all gone. Every last one of them!"

"I don't get it," Gordo said. "Who would want to steal a bunch of Doggy Day Care signs?"

Lizzie and Miranda looked at each other.

"Matt," Lizzie said immediately.

"Kate," Miranda said, just as fast.

Gordo put up his hands. "Okay, that's a dumb question. I take it back."

i say, *both* suspects are guilty until proven innocent in the Court of Lizzie!

34

Lizzie ran up and down the sidewalk on both sides of the street, checking trees. Sure enough, all of her flyers and posters had been torn down. Pieces of tape were still stuck to some of the trees.

"Definite sabotage," Gordo said, nodding.

"Maybe you're not supposed to put up signs on this street," Miranda suggested. "Hey, if Mayor Robertson is anything like his buddy Vice Principal Putney, he probably ripped them all down himself."

"No," Lizzie said. "There are other posters for yard sales and tutoring all over the place. I saw the same ones this morning."

"Guess we'll have to come up with a new way to advertise," Gordo said.

"Nope," Lizzie said, reaching into her knapsack. "I have backup." She pulled out her extra stack of flyers and a roll of tape. "Ta-da! Doggy Day Care lives!"

Lizzie, Gordo, and Miranda taped up flyers all the way back to Lizzie's house.

"That ought to do it," Lizzie said with satis-faction as she posted the last ad. "Hopefully, we haven't lost too many customers already."

"At least we have Baxter," Miranda said.

"True." Lizzie sighed. "But we're going to need *a lot* more clients to make enough money for the Hillridge Animal Shelter."

Just then, Kate breezed by on the sidewalk. Claire was striding right beside her. Behind them, the same geeky guys Lizzie had seen help-ing Kate at school earlier were now lugging the girls' books.

"Oh, hello, nonentities," Kate said, with a wave of her magenta-painted nails. "How's the pooper-scooper biz going?"

Miranda narrowed her eyes. "You should know, Kate. *You* took down all of Lizzie's signs, didn't you? If you ask me, *that's* the sort of busi-ness that stinks."

Kate twirled a long blond curl. "I have no idea *what* you're talking about," she said. "*I* didn't do anything." She smiled back at the AV guys. "Isn't that right?"

The two boys nodded their heads. "That's true," they both said, blushing and shuffling their sneakers.

Lizzie frowned. The two boys sounded honest when they'd answered. But she still smelled a rat.

So, Tweedle Dumb and Tweedle Dork are either Kate's alibis, or her accomplices . . . or *neither* if my little Tweedle Jerk brother is the guilty party . . . hmmm . . .

Ten seconds later, the little devil himself appeared. Matt came bounding over to them. His ever-silent friend Lanny was right beside him.

"So, how's it going, Sister CEO?" Matt asked. "Need my help yet?"

Lizzie grabbed Matt and Lanny both by the necks of their T-shirts.

"Hey!" Matt protested.

Lanny frowned and looked indignant.

"Did you little twerps take down my posters?" Lizzie demanded. "Because if you did, I'll tell Mom and Dad and you two will be on choke chains till junior high."

"I really think you should reconsider my offer, Lizzie," Matt said, trying to squirm out of her grasp. "Is this any way to treat a top consultant in the canine-management field?"

"This is all *extremely* entertaining," Kate broke in, "but Claire and I have shopping to do for an incredibly cool party you're not invited to. Ta-ta!" Then Kate, Claire, and their toady geek fan club were outie.

"Those girls are so—so—arrgh!" Miranda sputtered. "I can't believe you let them off the hook like that, Lizzie."

Lizzie dropped Matt and Lanny. The two boys scampered down the street like evil little mice.

"Don't worry," she told Miranda. "I'm not letting *anyone* off. I'm just choosing to deal with potential suspects later. Right now we have a business to run."

"Lizzie?" Mrs. McGuire called from the porch. "Phone for you! It's a lady calling about Doggy Day Care."

"See?" Lizzie said to Miranda and Gordo. "It'll be smooth sailing from now on."

"Aye, aye, Captain," Gordo said with a salute. "I sure hope you're right."


The next morning was Saturday. The first official day of spring break and Lizzie's Doggy Day Care business.

Lizzie was so excited, she woke up way before her alarm. She even beat Matt into the bathroom. "What was that you said yesterday?" Lizzie asked him, pretending to wrack her brain. "Ooooh, yeah. *Snoozers* are *losers*!" She shut the door in Matt's face.

Okay, that was totally rude and immature . . . but *so* satisfying!

As she showered, Lizzie went over some details in her head. So far, she had four doggy customers, including Baxter. People must have seen her flyers because she'd gotten three calls already.

All of her customers lived in the neighborhood, within easy walking distance. It had been a cinch to schedule walks and dog-sitting times over the phone.

Gordo had even promised to make a chart so that they could keep track of pet pickups and returns.

I am totally set, thought Lizzie happily. Running my own business is going to be a breeze!

# CHAPTER

6

"Okay, let's pick up the pace, doggies," Lizzie told the two lumbering sheepdogs she was walking. "We don't want to be late."

"You have to be firm with dogs, Lizzie," Gordo said. "Here, watch this. Daisy, Buttercup, *heel.*" He tugged on the dogs' leashes.

The huge, furry dogs started walking even slower. One of them stopped to sniff a fire hydrant.

Lizzie sighed and consulted the schedule on her notepad. So far, so good. They were due to meet up with Miranda at the corner of Elm and Brentwood in exactly five minutes.

"*Yikes!* Somebody *help me!*"

Lizzie's head snapped up and she saw Miranda running toward them, chased by a teeny, tiny dog that looked like a rat. The dog's studded leather leash trailed behind it.

Okay, revise that to meeting up with Miranda in five *seconds.*

Miranda raced up to Lizzie and grasped her shoulders. "Omigosh!" she gasped. "This dog is gonna kill me. Save me. *Please.*"

"Miranda, that's Scooter," said Lizzie calmly. "He wouldn't hurt a flea."

"Oh yeah?" Miranda crossed her arms. "Look at those fangs. He's a killer, I'm telling you."

"We'll trade you, Miranda," Gordo said. "You

can take Daisy and Buttercup here. They're just your speed."

Lizzie checked her notepad again. "We have to get these dogs settled in the backyard and keep an eye on them for the next two hours, then I leave to pick up a German shepherd named Donovan from the McNallys."

Miranda eyed Scooter. "Did you notice that beast is wearing a Harley-Davidson bandanna?"

"Look on the bright side," said Gordo. "He doesn't have any visible tattoos. And I'm pretty sure he's not carrying any weapons."

"Except those fangs," Miranda insisted.

A few minutes later, Lizzie, Miranda, Gordo, and their canine charges reached Lizzie's house.

Mrs. McGuire was waiting on the front porch with her hand to her forehead like she wasn't feeling well. She also seemed a bit frazzled.

"Lizzie, this Doggy Day Care business is completely out of hand," she said. "Didn't your father and I warn you about being *responsible*?"

"What's wrong, Mom?" Lizzie asked, puzzled. "We're doing just fine. Everything is totally under control."

"Control?" Mrs. McGuire cried. "You call what's going on in our backyard *under control*?"

Lizzie hurried to the backyard and opened the gate, followed closely by Gordo, Miranda, and the dogs. At least twenty people were back there—with their twenty dogs. All of them were waiting to hire Doggy Day Care.

"Oh no!" Lizzie gasped. "How did *this* happen? I only got three calls yesterday, and two more this morning."

"Well, let's get to work," Gordo said, shrugging. "We'll figure things out as we go along. We need some sort of system, that's all."

Lizzie pasted a smile on her face and walked up to an older woman in a red sweater. "Hi, I'm Lizzie," she said. "May I help you?"

"I certainly hope so," the woman said. She nodded at the boxer by her side. "This is

Duke and he needs a dog-sitter till three. I have a very important doctor's appointment."

"Um, sure," Lizzie said. "Is there anything special I should know about Duke?"

The woman looked around nervously. "Well, he doesn't like other dogs very much. But that nice little boy who knocked on my door and told me about your business said it wouldn't be a problem at all."

Lizzie's head began to spin.

**Matt! This is all his doing! The puny prince of publicity stunts has struck again!**

"Excuse me," Lizzie said through gritted teeth. "I'll be right back." She left Gordo and Miranda to deal with the customers and stomped into the house. Matt and Lanny were in front of the TV in the living room, surrounded by more dogs.

"Where's Mom?" Lizzie asked, trying to remain calm.

"Upstairs," Matt said, without turning around. He seemed fixated by a dog biscuit commercial with an obnoxiously cheery jingle. A half dozen of her clients' dogs had camped beside the couch. The canines seemed equally mesmerized by the TV commercial.

"She said she has a headache and is going to lie down for a little while," Matt informed her.

"Well, I need to talk to her right now," Lizzie said, starting toward the stairs. "It's an emergency."

"Not so fast," Matt said, holding out his palm to block her way. "Pay up."

"*Pay* you?" Lizzie cried. "For what? For wrecking my business and driving me totally crazy?"

"No, for our invaluable PR services," Matt said. "By the way, for you non-biz types, PR stands for Public Relations."

"M-O-O-O-M!" Lizzie shouted in desperation. There was no answer from upstairs.

"You know," Matt mused, gesturing to the TV screen, "the Buddy Bonz dog biscuit people could use some PR help, too. The jingle is catchy but that spokes-dog they have is all wrong."

I don't have time for this, Lizzie told herself. I have *responsibilities*. I can't just desert Gordo and Miranda with all those dogs.

She strode over and snapped off the TV. Matt and Lanny—and their canine companions—instantly slumped to the rug.

"Here's the 411, pest," Lizzie told her brother. "I'm going to be dog-sitting Vice Principal Putney's champion dog this afternoon. So get out in the backyard on the double and help me straighten this out. Now!"

Lizzie's next two hours as CEO of Doggy Day Care were more of a blur than a breeze. She sorted out dogs, schedules, and leashes, and tried to assure owners that everything was under control.

"We can't turn customers away," she told Gordo. "We need to raise as much money as possible for the animal shelter. But I don't see how we can manage all these dogs ourselves."

Gordo surveyed Lizzie's backyard. Dogs were everywhere, yapping and fighting and digging in Mrs. McGuire's garden. Miranda was standing on the deck with a pooper-scooper, her eyes squeezed tightly shut.

"I do like the doggies," she was telling herself. "I do, I do, I really do."

"Maybe we should hire some help," Gordo said, nodding toward Matt and Lanny, who were attempting to entertain a group of dogs using Mr. McGuire's cherished garden gnomes.

"*No!*" Lizzie cried, rushing toward her little brother and his friend. She rescued one of the brightly painted gnomes just as one of the dogs lifted its leg.

"You guys are *not* helping," Lizzie said. "You're making things worse."

"I thought you said a champion show dog was coming," Matt complained. "This is boring. We quit."

Lanny nodded in agreement.

"Quit?" Lizzie cried. "You can't quit. You caused this chaos."

Matt shrugged. "You can keep your sorry dog biz. Lanny and I have a much more lucrative fund-raising plan of our own."

"Fund-raising? For what?" asked Lizzie.

"For Matt and Lanny Charities, Inc.," said Matt with a snap of his fingers. Lanny nodded earnestly.

Charity? I'll give you charity. I'm allowing you both to remain on this planet—at least until all of these dogs are dog-gone!

Just as Matt and Lanny headed into the house,

a woman wearing a flowered muumuu and spongy pink curlers in her hair marched into the McGuires' yard.

"Uh-oh," Lizzie told Gordo in a low voice. "It's Ms. Harris from down the street."

"You mean the cat lady?" asked Gordo.

Lizzie nodded. "Yep. She's got tons of them."

Ms. Harris walked straight up to Lizzie. "Excuse me, young lady," she said. "But my precious kitties will be terrorized by having so many barking dogs so near. Do you have a permit for this business?"

Lizzie gulped. "Um . . . a permit?"

"I didn't think so," Ms. Harris said, crossing her arms. "Maybe I should make a call to Mayor Robertson's office to check on that."

Miranda suddenly slid up beside the cat lady. "Oh wow, did you say *cats*?" she asked. "I just loooove cats! How many do you have? What are all their names?"

The cat lady smiled down at Miranda. "I have

twenty-two beautiful kitties, my dear. It's always so nice to meet a fellow cat lover."

Lizzie sighed in relief. "Miranda's the greatest," she whispered to Gordo, as she watched her best girlfriend pull the cat lady away by her muumuu sleeve.

"Ms. Harris, don't worry!" called Lizzie. "We'll make sure the dogs stay in the yard!"

The cat lady turned and nodded distractedly. She was obviously still reciting all the names of her kitties to Miranda.

"Phew!" Lizzie said in relief. "That was a close one."

"Well, don't look now," Gordo said, "but here comes another neighbor. And he doesn't look happy, either."

A heavyset man in his late sixties with gray hair and white, bushy eyebrows had just walked through the gate. "Lizzie McGuire?" he said. "I need to talk to you."

Oh, no, Lizzie thought. What now? Mr.

Barney was usually pretty nice—even though he was *also* a little weird. He lived two houses away with a yard full of strange aerial fixtures. But he also had a very cool tree house. Once Matt got into trouble for trying to camp in it overnight.

"Lizzie, this dog business of yours is not good," Mr. Barney said. "All the barking is interfering with my transmissions from space."

Lizzie's eyes went wide. "Excuse me?" she squeaked.

Transmissions from space? Oh, of *course*! From the *aliens* journeying across the universe at the speed of light. So, will somebody out there please beam up Mr. Barney?

Lizzie looked to Gordo for help. After all, she told herself, he belongs to the Science Club, so he's got to be better equipped than me at dealing with *alien* issues.

"No worries, sir," Gordo said quickly. "I already have a foolproof plan to keep the dogs quiet. You won't hear a thing, I promise."

"Well, good," Mr. Barney said before turning to go. "Or you'll have to hear a thing or two—from *me*."

"Doggy Day Care is a total disaster!" Lizzie cried, as soon as Mr. Barney was gone. "How are we going to make all these dogs behave?"

"And what is Vice Principal Putney going to say when he gets here?" Miranda added, rejoining Lizzie and Gordo. She was wearing a huge red button that Ms. Harris had given her. It read: I ♥ CATS!

"I guess he'll say Kate will be getting that Community Helper Award," Lizzie said with a defeated sigh.

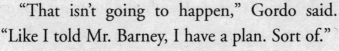

*McGuire, get a grip. There is no way you are going to let Kate beat you out. That thousand dollars is yours, yours, yours!*

"That isn't going to happen," Gordo said. "Like I told Mr. Barney, I have a plan. Sort of."

"What kind of plan?" Lizzie asked.

"Well, I've read that music can have a soothing effect on dogs," Gordo explained. "And since both my parents are shrinks, I think I can apply that to some of B.F. Skinner's behavioral theories."

"Who?" asked Miranda.

"B.F. Skinner," said Gordo. "He was able to prove that behavior can change through positive and negative reinforcements. It's called conditioning. I may be able to use his theories to train the dogs not to bark."

"In, like, an hour?" Lizzie asked. "We're desperate here."

Gordo frowned. "Well, it's a stretch," he said, "but if I can find a strong enough stimulus, I can train the dogs to respond faster. I'll be right back."

He ran into the house, leaving Lizzie and Miranda to deal with the growing canine craziness.

A few minutes later, Lizzie's mother appeared on the deck. She'd finally recovered from her headache and seemed to be adjusting fairly well to the new "doghouse." She'd even begun baking a batch of chocolate-chip cookies.

Holding out the cordless phone, Mrs. McGuire stepped over a yipping dachshund, and said, "Lizzie, phone call for you."

"Tell them we're booked up for Doggy Day

Care," Lizzie said waving her hand. "No more dogs."

"No, honey, it's Kate," Mrs. McGuire said. "She's just checking to see how things are going. Isn't that nice of her?"

Lizzie rolled her eyes. Kate was *never* nice. Her mom had no clue how much Kate had changed since grade school. These days, her former best friend was only polite to grown-ups.

"I'm sure Kate has some other reason for calling," Lizzie said to Miranda under her breath. "Whatever it is, it can't be good."

"Lizzie, hi!" Kate said sweetly when Lizzie took the phone. Then she quickly dropped her voice. "Listen up, McGuire," she said. "You can kiss all your little doggies bye-bye. Literally."

Then the Queen of Mean hung up.

"Who does she think she is, Cruella De Vil?" Miranda asked, when Lizzie repeated what Kate had said.

Lizzie sighed and headed into the house to

return the phone to the kitchen. On her way, she found Matt and Lanny and another bunch of dogs gaping at that stupid Buddy Bonz doggy biscuit commercial again.

It might have been déjà vu, Lizzie thought, if there wasn't something very different about the scene this time: *Gordo* was with them!

"How many times can you guys watch a dog biscuit commercial?" Lizzie asked, throwing up her hands.

"It's great," said Matt, staring at the screen. "I taped it so we can watch it over and over."

"What?" Lizzie cried. "That's the dumbest—"

"Shhh!" Gordo told her. "It's not the commercial. It's the jingle. It has a quieting effect on the dogs."

Lizzie noticed Matt and Lanny were also mesmerized. "A quieting effect on dogs *and* bratty little kids," she muttered under her breath.

"Lizzie, I need to use your computer," Gordo said. "I want to log onto the Buddy Bonz Web site and download this jingle into my new cell phone. My parents gave it to me for emergencies."

"Hello? We're in an *emergency* situation *right now*," Lizzie said. "Do you think maybe you could *wait* to download a stupid doggy treat jingle?"

Just then, the cordless phone rang in Lizzie's hand. She was so tense she nearly jumped through the ceiling.

"Hello, Lizzie?" the boy on the other end said. "This is Joey McNally. Forget about picking up our German shepherd Donovan today, okay?"

"Oh no!" Lizzie said. "Why?"

"Um, well . . ." Joey said, sounding guilty. "Something else came up."

Lizzie frowned as the phone rang again. It was another owner calling to cancel.

"Sorry, I got a better deal," the girl told her.

A better deal? Lizzie thought. Doggy Day Care only charges five dollars per hour of sitting! Who could be offering less than that?

Soon the doorbell began to ring, too. People were arriving to pick up their dogs—way too early!

Hey, what's going on? Where are all my customers going—and *why*? Uh-oh, my booming Doggy Day Care biz is becoming a bust!

CHAPTER

8

"That does it!" Lizzie told Miranda after another customer arrived to pick up her dog. "I'm going to follow the next person who cancels and see where he or she goes."

"You mean you're going to put a *tail* on them?" Miranda asked with a raised eyebrow. Then she smiled.

Lizzie sighed. "Ha-ha," she said weakly.

"Hey, guys!" Gordo called from the yard. "Check this out!"

Lizzie and Miranda rushed through the sliding

door and onto the wooden deck. "What?" Lizzie said. "Are our customers coming back?"

"Well, no," Gordo said. "But I'm making some progress here with the conditioned behavioral response training. Sort of. Did you notice that things are getting quieter already?"

"That's probably because a lot of the dogs are leaving, Gordo," Miranda said. "Or haven't you noticed?"

Gordo ignored her. He was too busy concentrating on his training. "Okay, this is how it works," he said. "I'll use Coal here as an example. She's the little black poodle over there, running around in circles and barking."

As Lizzie and Miranda watched, Gordo punched some buttons on his cell phone. "I'm using the programmable ring-test function," he explained. "That way, I can play the Buddy Bonz doggy treat jingle whenever I want."

The annoying tune began to play.

Coal immediately stopped barking and sat in

front of Gordo—in the middle of a bunch of daffodils.

"Note that I'm holding up a Buddy Bonz treat at the same time as I play the jingle," Gordo said, taking a dog biscuit from his pocket.

"Right," Lizzie said. She'd bought the treats the day before for her doggie clientele. "Um, Gordo, where is this all going?"

"Yeah, can you speed it up a little?" Miranda said. "Before the doorbell starts ringing again."

"The treat is the reward, you see," Gordo said. "And the jingle is the stimulus. The stimulus combined with the reward produces a conditioned response. . . ."

Lizzie looked around the yard. By now, all the dogs had stopped barking. They were all sitting quietly.

"Amazing," Miranda said. "They're, like, trying to outdo each other, behaving and being quiet for a treat."

*Ding-dong!*

Lizzie frowned. "That's the doorbell again." She ran to answer it, followed by Miranda. Gordo stayed behind, absorbed in working with his doggy test subjects.

"Bring back more Buddy Bonz treats!" he called after the girls. "I'm about to run out!"

Lizzie hurried through the house and threw open the front door. Two teenage twin sisters from a few blocks away, Kailey and Lauren Williams, were standing on the porch.

"Um, hi, Lizzie," Lauren said. "We need to pick up Coal."

"Yeah," Kailey said, nodding hard. "Our mom says she has to come home. We're . . . um . . . going to . . ."

"Take her to the park," Lauren filled in quickly. "Right now. So, we don't need you to dog-sit anymore."

"But here's some money for the time she was here," Kailey offered, holding out five dollars.

Lizzie sighed. "Thanks, guys," she said, taking

it. "This money is going to a good cause."

Miranda had already brought the little black poodle around from the backyard. Coal was still licking her chops from the Buddy Bonz treat.

"She may not be very hungry," Lizzie called after the girls as they left.

Lizzie closed the door and waited a few seconds. "Okay," she told Miranda. "I'm going to follow them."

"I'm going with you," said Miranda.

The two left Lizzie's house and began to tail Kailey, Lauren, and Coal.

"Where do you think they're going?" Miranda whispered.

"I don't know," Lizzie said grimly. "But they've already passed their house. And the park is in the other direction."

**Somebody throw me a bone here!**

Lizzie and Miranda trailed their ex-clients across the neighborhood—and straight to a very familiar house.

"Kate!" Lizzie said, narrowing her eyes. "I should have known."

"Now we know why she told you to kiss the puppies good-bye," said Miranda angrily.

Lizzie's mouth dropped open. "Half of our Doggy Day Care clients are in her front yard!" she said.

"Well, obviously she's abandoned her lame-o wannabe booster-board fund-raiser," Miranda said. "Guess it tanked big-time."

"So, she's resorting to *this*?" Lizzie cried.

Kate, Claire, and the rest of the cheer queens had set up an elaborate booth in the Sanderses' huge front yard. The booth was decorated in blue and white, the Hillridge Junior High colors. And there was a large sign advertising Kate's new fund-raiser.

> **Pamper Your Pooch**
> **with**
> **DOG WALKS BY KATE**
> **$4 an hour**
> **Sign up now**
> **and receive**
> **a special bonus!**

Lizzie felt her face grow hot. "Kate *stole* my dog-walking idea!" she said to Miranda. "And she's charging a dollar less!"

"And she's got those AV geeks who are crushin' on the cheerleaders to do the dog-walking for her!" Miranda pointed out.

"It gets worse," Lizzie moaned. "That special bonus they're offering? Little blue-and-white hats and 'accessories' designed for Fido!"

"That's sad," Miranda said, shaking her head. "*Very* sad."

"But smart," Lizzie said. "No wonder so many of our customers left. How can I compete with Kate?"

Miranda shrugged. "Same way she did. Go low. Like a snake."

Lizzie looked back at the booth. There were lots of people and dogs standing around it. If she confronted Kate right now, she would cause an ugly scene. And that wouldn't be good for business, thought Lizzie, Kate's *or* Doggy Day Care's.

Lizzie took a deep breath. Be strong, she told herself. Think long-term business strategy. You have a whole week left to make money for the Hillridge Animal Shelter.

I can beat Kate Sanders at her own game—and win the Community Helper Award, too. Why? Because it's a dog-eat-dog world. *Woof!*

"Come on," Lizzie said to Miranda. "We're leaving."

"Huh?" Miranda asked. "But what about Kate?" She nodded toward the busy booth. Dogs were waiting for walks in their little blue-and-white hats. Most of the dogs were trying to chew them off.

"You take this side of the street," she told Miranda. "I'll take the other. We're going to tell everyone headed toward Kate's house that our business is for charity—*and* we're going to charge only three dollars. Then tonight we'll make new flyers and distribute them. And, I can't believe I'm saying this, but I might even stoop to asking Matt and Lanny to help."

"If you say so, boss," Miranda said. "But I don't know if three bucks per hour is really worth the effort."

"Oh, it will be," Lizzie said. "You can trust me on that."

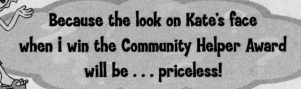

When Lizzie and Miranda finally arrived back at Lizzie's house—after a stop at the local pet store to buy a big bag of Buddy Bonz—they found Gordo in the kitchen. He was helping himself to a plate of Mrs. McGuire's freshly baked chocolate-chip cookies.

"Gordo," Lizzie said, "why aren't you in the backyard with the dogs?"

"Oh, I took a little break from my Buddy Bonz jingle-and-biscuit experiment," Gordo said. "Right after Vice Principal Putney dropped off Baxter."

Lizzie sighed. I want a break, too, she thought. As soon as I've given all those dogs some water and gathered their leashes and—

"Whoa!" Lizzie blurted out. "Wait just a sec, Gordo. Are you saying Baxter's here *already*?"

"Relax, Lizzie," Gordo said. "Vice Principal Putney was totally impressed by the unusually quiet facilities. And we had a nice, long chat about Baxter."

"Wonderful," Lizzie said. Her head was beginning to hurt.

"Vice Principal Putney has Baxter on a very expensive, strictly high-protein diet," Gordo went on. "He brought Baxter's regular food in those Tupperware containers over there. Baxter won't eat anything else."

"Mmmhmm," Lizzie said, not really paying attention. Gordo was right. The backyard facilities sure *were* unusually quiet.

"In fact, Baxter's food smells like filet mignon to me," Gordo added. "I was almost tempted to try it. And Vice Principal Putney warned me about those raunchy Buddy Bonz treats. As far as treats go, Baxter will only eat his bacon-flavored vitamin biscuits."

"Fascinating," Lizzie said. "Gordo, I can't believe I'm saying this. But it's way *too* quiet back there. It doesn't seem right."

Lizzie worriedly left the kitchen, moved to the back door, and stepped onto the deck.

"Oh, no," she said, not wanting to believe her eyes. "It can't be."

But it was. The gate to the backyard was standing open—and all the dogs were gone!

"Impossible!" Lizzie cried. "I made sure that gate was latched this morning after Mr. Barney left. Those dogs couldn't *possibly* escape!"

"Um, Lizzie, I hate to break this to you," Miranda said. "But it looks like they *did*."

"I'm really, really sorry, Lizzie," Gordo said. He was shaking his head and rubbing the back of his neck. He seemed even more upset than Lizzie. "I was only in the house for about ten minutes."

"That's okay, Gordo," Lizzie said with a sigh. "I should have been here. It was my idea."

So now I guess I should change my middle name to Lizzie ir-responsible McGuire. That's the way it should be printed on my Community *Loser* Award certificate.

"Maybe the dogs haven't gotten too far," Miranda said hopefully.

The spring breeze had grown pretty strong and Lizzie's hair began whipping around her face. She pulled a band from her jeans pocket and tied it back.

"We'd better start looking," Lizzie said. Then she hurried through the yard to the gate with Miranda and Gordo behind her.

"Do you think one of the dogs could have opened this gate by accident?" Miranda asked. "I bet it was that nasty Scooter. I told you guys he was trouble."

"Scooter couldn't jump that high," said Gordo. "Besides, just bumping the latch by accident wouldn't open the gate. This is a fork latch. A person has to pull down pretty firmly on it to make it release."

Lizzie knelt down and looked carefully at the ground by the gate. "There are so many paw prints here I can't find any fresh footprints," she said.

"Well, who was in this yard today?" Miranda asked.

Lizzie threw up her hands. "Just about everyone in the neighborhood who owns a dog."

"Or a cat," Miranda said. "You're forgetting the cat lady."

"And Mr. Barney, the alien guy," Gordo added.

Lizzie nodded. "They both complained about the noise," she said. "So either one of them might want to wreck Doggy Day Care."

"But Matt wrecked your posters because you wouldn't cut him in for a share of the profits, and Kate tried to steal your business," Miranda pointed out. "That means they have motives, too."

"Guys," Gordo broke in. "We may be on the

right track here, but the first order of business is to find the dogs. Right?"

"Right," Lizzie and Miranda said together. But as they and Gordo left the yard, latching the gate carefully, Lizzie glanced back.

"I think I see something stuck on that gate!" she told her friends. She looked more closely. *Tape!* she realized. And there was a tiny piece of white paper stuck to it. But the rest of the note, if that's what it had been, was gone.

"Rats," Lizzie said. "That could have been a clue."

"Maybe it was a ransom note left by the dog-napper," Miranda said. "You know, like 'Leave five million dollars in an envelope near the bus stop or you'll never see your doggies again.'"

"Don't even go there," Lizzie said. "Because you know somebody might—"

Suddenly, she spotted a piece of white paper fluttering in the middle of the street. "The note!" she cried, running after it. The strong breeze blew it all the way down the block. When she finally reached down to grab it, she felt a sudden, strong spray of water.

"H-hey!" Lizzie sputtered, whirling around. She was all wet! A group of little boys from the neighborhood were standing behind her, laughing their heads off. Two of them carried enormous Super Soakers.

"We got you! We got you!" the oldest boy cried. Then the whole group went running off in search of their next victim.

Things *could* be worse. i could have gone into the babysitting business and been stuck dealing with those bratty little Mini Matts!

Lizzie looked down at the paper in her hand. It was totally Super Soaked. Oh, no! she thought. My one big clue is ruined!

Gordo and Miranda came rushing up. "Wow, they really did get you," Miranda said.

"*And* the note," Lizzie said. "Parts of it are totally smeared." She read the note—or what was left of it—to her friends:

```
. . . . . . . . . . . SAY GOOD-BYE.
TO . . . . THE DOG . . . . . . . . . . .          .
        . . . . . . . . . . .
. . . KEEP . . . . QUIET . . . . . . . . . . .
        . . . . . . . . . . .
```

"This is terrible," Lizzie said. "It sounds like the dogs are in danger. We have to save them!"

"Do you think this was supposed to be some kind of ransom note? Or just a threat?" Gordo asked, looking at the note again. "It's hard to tell with the words all smudged."

"Well, whatever it is, it doesn't sound good," Miranda said.

"Gordo, think. Who came into the yard after Miranda and I left?" Lizzie asked.

Gordo frowned. "After you left . . ."

"Yes, think, Gordo. Think!" Lizzie pressed.

"Oh, yeah," Gordo remembered. "Mr. Barney and the cat lady both complained about the barking again. It was before I got my experiment working really well."

"That's pretty important," Lizzie said. "The note says 'keep . . . quiet . . .' So, those two are definitely suspects. But would either of them really have left a note like that?"

"And what about Matt and Kate?" Miranda said. "They could have snuck into the yard from the sidewalk when Gordo was inside the house on his cookie break. Either of them would have left a note like that. Matt likes to bug you, Lizzie. And Kate actually called to say good-bye to the puppies."

"Kate's a real possibility," Lizzie said. "Matt is, too."

"But we stopped by the pet store to get more doggy treats. She could have done it then. Or she could have gotten one of the AV guys to let our dogs out," Miranda argued. "If they're walking all those dogs for Kate, they'd probably do anything for her."

"And then there's Matt," said Lizzie.

Gordo scratched his head. "Well, Matt left the house with Lanny before you two got back."

"Where did he go?" asked Lizzie.

"Something about research for Matt and Lanny Charities, Inc.," said Gordo.

Lizzie rolled her eyes at her stupid brother's stupid schemes and looked back down at the note again. It was the best clue they had. The note had been written in black Magic Marker. And except for the smudged letters, it was very neatly block printed.

"Do you recognize the handwriting?" Miranda asked.

"Well, it's not Matt's," Lizzie said. "His

writing looks like chicken scratch. These letters are practically perfect. It looks like a grown-up wrote this."

Just then, Gordo's cell phone rang. He answered it. "Oh, hi, Ms. Putney. . . . Absolutely. Everything's going just *great* with Baxter. I'm glad Vice Principal Putney gave you my cell phone number. In case of any, uh . . . emergency." Gordo met Lizzie's panicked eyes. "Which is highly unlikely, of course."

Lizzie gulped nervously and glanced at her watch. It was almost three o'clock—and Vice Principal Putney's sister would be arriving at the house at six!

Maybe she's calling to say she'll be late, Lizzie thought hopefully. Please, please, oh, please—

"Sure, Ms. Putney," she heard Gordo say. "See you at six sharp."

Lizzie dropped onto the sidewalk and put her soggy head in her wet hands. "We're doomed!" she wailed.

CHAPTER

10

"Don't worry, Lizzie," Miranda said. She sat down next to Lizzie and put an arm around her. "We can solve this crime by suppertime!"

Lizzie just groaned.

"Lizzie, Miranda's right," Gordo said. "We'll find the dogs *and* the kidnapper before six. You know why?"

Lizzie looked up. "Why?" she asked, ready to cry.

Gordo did a little spin. "Because *I* have a *plan.*"

Lizzie sighed. "Okay, let's hear it," she said.

"We can call the dogs back to us with the Buddy Bonz dog biscuit jingle," Gordo said. "I downloaded it into my cell phone, remember?"

"Not bad, Gordo," Miranda said, impressed.

"Better than not bad," said Lizzie. "That idea totally rocks." Then she actually smiled.

Gordo was so proud of himself, he launched right into Scientist Speak: "From the brief behavioral experiments I conducted with the Doggy Day Care subjects in your backyard and the way they drooled for Buddy Bonz treats, I can safely conclude that the catchy jingle will bring them running."

"I thought they just sat down and stopped barking," Miranda said.

"Work with me here, okay, Miranda?" Gordo said.

"Right," Miranda said. "Sorry."

"When I press the tone test function on my cell phone, the dogs will hear the Buddy Bonz customized ring. With luck, they'll return to Lizzie's backyard—for their treat."

They lost no time testing Gordo's theory. Empty leashes in hand, they ran though the neighborhood, following paw prints as Gordo rang his cell phone.

"Wait a minute," Lizzie said finally. "Is anyone else noticing a pattern here?"

Gordo and Miranda looked at each other. "What are you talking about, Lizzie?" Miranda asked.

Lizzie gestured to the ground. "We've been picking up paw prints," she said. "Trails and trails of them. At first, they seemed to be going in circles, but now they're all heading to the same place." She pointed down the street.

Gordo held up his cell phone and pushed the tone test button. "My battery's starting to die," he said, frowning. "But I think I hear the sound of dogs barking."

Lizzie nodded, and the three tried to follow

the sound. "The barking's getting louder," she whispered. "Hear it?"

Miranda and Gordo nodded.

"I think it's coming from behind that house at the end of the street," Miranda said. "So who lives in that house?"

"Ms. Harris. The cat lady," Lizzie said. "*Now* we know who let the dogs out!"

Lizzie, Miranda, and Gordo ran toward Ms. Harris's house.

"Around back," said Lizzie.

"Whoa!" cried Miranda when they got there.

Ms. Harris was running around in her big backyard. She looked frantic—and totally furious! Twenty-one of her twenty-two kitties had all climbed up her oak tree, and they were hissing angrily. The only kitty not up that tree was running around the backyard, leading a pack of dogs on a merry chase.

"Guys, we've found them!" Lizzie cried excitedly. "We've found our dogs—and our dognapper!"

But she stopped short in her tracks when the cat lady spotted her. The woman's face grew red, then purple with anger. "Get these mutts out of my yard *now*!" Ms. Harris bellowed. "Or I'm calling the cops!"

"Maybe we should just take the dogs and talk to this suspect later," Gordo advised, catching up to Lizzie. "She looks a bit . . . *unglued*."

"Right," Miranda said. "I'd take dealing with Scooter over the cat lady any day."

"Okay, Ms. Harris," Lizzie said, waving as she and her friends began to corral and leash up the hyper dogs. "We're leaving. Right now."

"Gordo, use your cell phone," Miranda hissed. "Make the dogs sit down and shut up now!"

"Sorry," Gordo said. "I think my battery's dead."

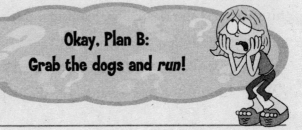

Okay, Plan B:
Grab the dogs and *run*!

Ten minutes later, Lizzie, Gordo, and Miranda were flopping in relief on the grass in the McGuires' backyard, still panting hard.

"I can't believe we got all the dogs back here so fast," Lizzie said. "Good job, guys."

"We did close and latch the gate behind us, right?" Gordo said, sitting up quickly.

Lizzie closed her eyes. "Yes, Gordo," she said. "Believe me, we did."

"So what are we going to do about the cat lady?" Miranda asked. "Do we have to go back there?"

"No," Lizzie said. "I'm scratching her off the suspect list. I don't think she'd want to let the dogs out. And we can't have a suspect with a less-than-zero motive."

"The dogs must have chased one of her cats back to her yard," Gordo agreed. "Someone *else* let them out."

But who? Lizzie wondered with a sigh.

"I better clean up the yard before Vice

Principal Putney's sister comes to pick up Baxter," Lizzie said. Then she did a double take. "Wait a minute. Where *is* Baxter?"

Somebody tell me i'm dreaming . . . because if Mr. Putney's dog is missing, my life will become a total nightmare!

CHAPTER

11

"Baxter's missing!" Lizzie cried, running back to Miranda and Gordo. "I don't see him in the yard anywhere!"

"Are you sure?" asked Gordo.

"Of course I'm sure!" exclaimed Lizzie.

"Not good," said Gordo.

Miranda didn't say anything. She just turned very pale.

"I can't believe this," Lizzie said. "We found all the dogs except Vice Principal Putney's champion show dog!"

Actually, that *is* pretty believable. Does anything *ever* go right when you tell people how mature and responsible you are?

"Look, Baxter must still be out there somewhere," Miranda said. "A huge, gold-colored dog is hard to hide. Too bad we didn't lose Scooter instead."

At that very moment, Miranda's favorite little rat-dog was furiously digging a huge hole in Mrs. McGuire's vegetable garden. When he heard his name, he stopped and snarled in Miranda's direction.

"Well, at least we can use the Buddy Bonz jingle to track Baxter down," Lizzie said. "Gordo, is your cell phone recharged yet?"

"Sorry, Lizzie," Gordo said. "But Baxter was the only dog that didn't respond to the jingle."

"What?" Lizzie cried. "Why not?"

Gordo shrugged. "Mr. Putney's got Baxter on an expensive high-protein diet. Like I told you earlier, his food smelled like filet mignon—it even made *me* drool. So, it's no surprise Buddy Bonz's cheap charms held no appeal for Baxter as a response reward."

How can a dog turn up his nose at a dog biscuit? it would be like me passing up chocolate-chip cookies—totally not possible!

"Maybe we should look at the note again," Gordo suggested. "It's our only real clue so far."

"If we can find the person who wrote it, we might find Baxter," Miranda agreed.

Lizzie took the smeared note from her jeans pocket. "I have it memorized," she said. "But there's something I've been thinking."

She took a deep breath. "I know there are words missing," she said. "But look at this. It says '*the* dog.' *One* dog."

"Baxter," Gordo said.

Lizzie nodded. "Do you think that means the culprit just wanted Baxter? It sounds that way to me."

"You mean he or she let the other dogs out by accident?" Miranda asked.

"Or as a *distraction* so he or she could get away with Baxter," Lizzie said. "Which is exactly what the dognapper did."

"Really bad, Lizzie," Miranda said. "By now the guilty party could be pretty far away."

Lizzie tried not to think about the wrath of Vice Principal Putney. How many months . . . years . . . no, make that *decades* of detention would she have to serve for losing his prize pooch? she wondered.

*But* . . . she still had a few suspects left. Kate, for one. The Queen of Mean was clearly determined to win the Community Helper Award, and not just for the cash prize.

She wants to beat me, Lizzie realized. Kate can't stand to have me be better than her at anything. She'd almost broken her foot in gym class trying to prove she was better than me at rhythmic gymnastics, which she wasn't.

But Lizzie knew she couldn't confront Kate about Baxter until she was absolutely sure. Dognapping was a pretty serious crime, and would Kate really want to risk getting caught stealing—or putting anyone up to stealing—Vice Principal Putney's pet? That seemed pretty far out there, even for Kate. But Lizzie wasn't ruling it out.

They'd *already* ruled out Ms. Harris as a suspect. "But what about crazy Mr. Barney?" Lizzie murmured aloud.

"What's that?" asked Miranda.

Lizzie turned to Miranda and Gordo. "I think we should talk to Mr. Barney right now," she said firmly. "Maybe he's not really crazy."

"That's possible," Gordo said. "Maybe he was just pretending to complain about the barking interrupting his 'transmissions from space' while he cased the joint."

"Yeah," Miranda joked, "he's probably trying to beam Baxter up to the alien spaceship right now."

"And if we don't find Vice Principal Putney's dog in two hours, I'm going to want to be *on* that spaceship," said Lizzie.

"Well, one thing's for sure," Miranda said. "Mr. Barney might be just weird enough to hold a champion dog for ransom."

Lizzie ran into the house and found her father reading a magazine in the family room. "Dad, I know the dogs are my responsibility and everything," she said, "but I need you to do me a really big favor. Really big."

Once Mr. McGuire agreed to sit out on the backyard deck and watch over the dogs while she was gone, Lizzie grabbed Miranda and Gordo.

"Let's go!" she cried.

"Maybe we should search Mr. Barney's yard first," Lizzie told her friends when they reached his house. "Baxter could be around outside somewhere."

"Okay, let's split up," Gordo said.

"No way," Miranda said. "This place is creepy."

Lizzie looked around. Miranda was right. There were all kinds of wires and electronic equipment everywhere.

"He's definitely tracking something," Gordo said, frowning. "That looks like some sort of satellite device over there."

"Let's start with the tree house," Lizzie suggested nervously.

"Lizzie," Gordo said, "do you really think Mr. Barney would be hiding Baxter in a *tree house*?"

"No," Lizzie said. "But we might have a better view of everything from up there."

"Good point," Gordo admitted. "Lead on."

"Guys," Miranda said, her voice high and

tight. "Do you get the feeling that someone is watching us?"

Lizzie gazed around the yard again. "Sort of," she said.

Just as she spoke, a shadow fell across the grass. She turned slowly around—and came to face-to-face with Mr. Barney, who did not look happy. Not one bit.

Busted!

Lizzie gulped. "M-Mr. Barney," she said. "Um, hi!"

Mr. Barney took a step closer. He's a lot taller than I remember, Lizzie thought.

"We can explain, Mr. Barney," Miranda said. "Hey, do you have cats? What are their names?"

"Nice try," Gordo muttered.

"Listen, it worked once," Miranda whispered.

"Would you kids mind telling me what you're doing on my property?" Mr. Barney demanded. "I don't get many visitors."

Just aliens, Lizzie almost blurted out.

And *now* would be an excellent time for them to show up. Yoo-hoo! E.T.! Little green Martians! Anybody? Come on down!

"You're snooping around, aren't you?" Mr. Barney said.

Gordo straightened his shoulders. "And it looks as if you do quite a bit of snooping yourself, too, sir," he said.

Mr. Barney raised his bushy white eyebrows. "Excuse me, young man?" he said.

"We're not actually snooping, Mr. Barney," Lizzie spoke up quickly. "You see, we have this, um, big science fair coming up, and we thought since you have so many interesting pieces of metal in your yard that you might be able to help us with our, uh—"

"Research on magnetic force fields," Gordo finished quickly.

"Kids," Mr. Barney said, "I have no idea what you're getting at here."

"We're studying aliens, too," Miranda added. "And you said all the dog barking was disturbing your communications with them, so we figured the aliens might be landing here soon and—"

"*Aliens?*" Mr. Barney boomed. "Okay, that's it! One of you kids better start telling me the truth. And now would be a *very* good time."

This is seriously not going well, Lizzie thought. We're the ones who are supposed to be asking the questions. After all, Mr. Barney is suspected of being a dognapper! . . . On the other hand, their suspect *had* caught them red-handed sneaking around his yard.

Lizzie sighed in defeat. At this point, honesty was probably the best policy, she decided.

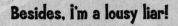

**Besides, i'm a lousy liar!**

Lizzie took a deep breath and began to tell Mr. Barney the whole story. Miranda and Gordo jumped in to help in parts. He listened quietly, frowning, until they had finished.

"So, Mr. Barney," Lizzie said. "*Did* you steal Baxter? And are you really trying to contact aliens?"

At first Mr. Barney looked angry. Then he seemed confused. Finally, he started to laugh.

"Young lady, you must learn to listen a little closer to *exactly* what people say, and what I said was 'transmissions from *space*.' I never said a thing about aliens or little green men or anything like it."

"Phew," Miranda said.

"All these antennas and wires are here because I'm a ham-radio operator," Mr. Barney went on. "I can pick up radio signals from all over the country. In an emergency, I'd be able to communicate with other operators and help people in our neighborhood."

"But what about all this satellite equipment, sir?" Gordo said. "It looks pretty advanced."

"Well now, that's where the *space* transmissions come in," Mr. Barney said. "I'm a retired park ranger, you see. I used to rescue animals and then track them through tiny transmitters for a wildlife-tracking satellite. Even though I live in the suburbs now, I still check in on my old animal friends every Saturday morning through satellite technology. My tracking system includes a very delicate audio signal, and all that dog barking was so loud, I couldn't hear a thing."

"You rescued animals?" Lizzie said, impressed.

Okay, so how bad do I feel about accusing Mr. Barney of being a dognapper *now*? Can this get any worse?

"We're trying to rescue animals, too," Lizzie explained. "By raising money for the Hillridge Animal Shelter."

"Well, that's a very worthy cause," Mr. Barney said. "And I certainly hope you find Baxter. I'm afraid I haven't seen him."

"Thanks anyway, Mr. Barney," Lizzie said. "And we're sorry for bothering you. But we have to get back to our case right now. We have a missing dog to find!"

Mr. Barney nodded and gave Lizzie and her friends a wave as he headed back into his house. "Good luck," he called.

Thanks, Lizzie thought. We're sure going to need it.

"**Y**ikes," Lizzie said, checking her watch. She, Gordo, and Miranda were standing on the sidewalk outside Mr. Barney's house. "It's after five already. We now have exactly fifty-two minutes left to retrieve our missing retriever."

"Maybe we should just spend that time practicing how we're going to tell Vice Principal Putney's sister that Baxter is gone," said Miranda.

Lizzie sighed. "You mean, how *I'm* going to tell her. Baxter was *my* responsibility."

"No, Lizzie," Gordo said. "I feel responsible, too."

"Yeah, and we're a *team*, remember," said Miranda. "*Team* Doggy Day Care. Gordo and I would never let you take the rap alone. Friends don't do that to each other, Lizzie."

Once again, Lizzie felt like she was going to cry.

"It's really my fault anyway," Gordo continued. "I shouldn't have taken that cookie break. If I'd been watching the yard, I might have seen who opened that gate. Or Matt might have, if he hadn't gone to the library."

"Whoa, Gordo," Lizzie said. "Did you just say Matt went to the *library*?"

"Yeah," said Gordo with a shrug. "Matt said that he and Lanny were leaving because they had to do some 'important research' for their big fund-raising project."

"*Library* research?" said Lizzie. "On the first day of spring break?"

Gordo shrugged.

"What are you thinking, Lizzie?" asked Miranda.

"Just this: Matt's no bookworm," said Lizzie narrowing her eyes. "He's just a worm."

"Excuse me?" said Miranda.

"Gordo, are you telling me my mother bought that story?" asked Lizzie, starting to walk quickly toward her house.

"Well, she was upstairs at the time," Gordo said. "And your dad was out running an errand. So, Lanny and Matt wrote a note and left it on the fridge."

"Gordo, give me your cell phone," Lizzie said. "Quick!"

"Here you go," Gordo said. "But the battery won't last long. It's not fully charged."

Lizzie punched in her home number. "Hello, Mom?" she said into the phone. "Is Matt there?"

"No, honey," Mrs. McGuire said. "He and Lanny are still at the library."

"Where are you right now?" Lizzie asked. "Are you in the kitchen?"

"Yes," Mrs. McGuire said. "Lizzie, is anything wrong?"

"Everything's fine, Mom," Lizzie said quickly. Then she remembered what Mr. Barney had told her—about paying attention to *exactly* what people say. "Mom, would you please tell me *exactly* what the note says—the one that Matt left you."

"Okay," said Mrs. McGuire. "I took it off the fridge but it's around here somewhere—oh, here it is. The note reads, 'Gone to do some fundraising research. Back soon. Lanny and Matt.'"

So, Lizzie thought, it doesn't *exactly* say they're at the library. Both Gordo and her mother just assumed it. She shook her head. Mr. Barney was right. It's important to *listen* to *exactly* what people say, especially when you're dealing with a little boy who's an evil genius!

"You know, that Lanny has beautiful handwriting," Mrs. McGuire mused. "Very mature. I wish your brother could print as well as he does."

Handwriting? Lanny? Lizzie thought. She covered the cell phone mouthpiece and turned to Miranda and Gordo. "I forgot all about *Lanny*!" she whispered. "*He* could have written that note on the gate!"

Of course, Lizzie had never actually *seen* Lanny's penmanship. "Mom, is their note written in black Magic Marker, by any chance? And in neat block letters."

"Yes, it is. Why?" asked Mrs. McGuire.

"No reason," she told her mother quickly. *Except* that Matt and Lanny left a note that has an awful lot in common with the dognapper's note, Lizzie added to herself. "We'll check up on Matt for you while we're out. Bye, Mom!"

Just as she hung up, a large public bus went by with a Buddy Bonz ad on the side.

"Don't look, Lizzie," Miranda advised. "It'll just make you feel worse."

But Lizzie shook her head. "We've got to catch

that bus," she told Gordo and Miranda. "I'll explain later, okay?"

The three of them raced to the bus stop at the end of the block. The bus was just about to pull away. Lizzie pounded on the door. "Excuse me!" she called.

The driver opened the door again. "One dollar," he said. "Exact change, please."

"Have you by any chance seen two little boys with a big gold dog on your route today?" Lizzie asked. "One of them has spiky hair. The other doesn't speak."

The bus driver shrugged. "A couple of kids like that tried to get on my bus a few hours ago," he said. "Wanted to go downtown to the Hillridge Hotel. But only guide dogs are allowed on public buses, so I told the kids to hoof it. The spiky-headed one tried to bribe me, can you believe it?"

"Oh, I believe it," Lizzie said.

"So, are you getting on or what?" the driver asked. "I don't have all day."

"Neither do we," Lizzie said as she, Miranda, and Gordo jumped onto the bus. "But I sure wish we did!"

On the ride downtown, Lizzie told her friends her theory: that Matt and Lanny had dognapped Baxter.

"But why?" Miranda asked.

Lizzie sat back in the seat and crossed her arms. On this she was clueless. "Just to make my life difficult, I guess," she said. "And trust me, when I get my hands on that little—"

Suddenly, she noticed another Buddy Bonz ad above one of the bus windows. It showed a droopy-looking basset hound with one paw draped over a box of dog biscuits.

Matt's right, Lizzie couldn't help thinking. The Buddy Bonz people do need a new spokes-dog. That one's pretty homely. Then she took a closer look at the advertisement. Underneath the photo the text read:

> ## HELP US FIND
> ## OUR NEW BUDDY!
>
> Do you have a canine pal who's
> special enough to be the new Buddy Bonz
> dog? If you think your pet has what it
> takes, bring him or her to the
> Hillridge Hotel between 12 and 6 P.M.
> on any Saturday this month!
> The winner will receive a $10,000
> Buddy Bonz appearance contract
> and a lifetime supply of Buddy Bonz.
> All other entrants in the
> **FIND OUR NEW BUDDY**
> contest search will receive a free bag
> of doggy-delicious Buddy Bonz!

"Miranda, Gordo, check this out!" Lizzie said. "We've solved our case!"

Gordo gave a low whistle. "Looks like Matt and Lanny are going to be doing a lot of free dog-walking this week."

"Maybe for the rest of their tormented little lives," Miranda agreed.

"You can bet on it," Lizzie said.

So, i guess it turns out Sneaky Sibling Suspect and Perfect Penmanship Pal had a pretty sweet motive. Driving me buggy was just an added bonus.

"Last stop, Hillridge Hotel!" the driver called.

The bus stopped in front of a large hotel at the end of the street near the Hillridge Civic Center. A big banner out front read: WELCOME BUDDY BONZ DOG BISCUIT FANS!

Gordo grinned. "Guess at this point all signs lead to Matt and Lanny," he said, "and more importantly . . . *Baxter*."

"Look at all these people!" Lizzie said.

"And *dogs*," Miranda added, with a gulp.

Lizzie, Miranda, and Gordo had just stepped into the busy lobby of the Hillridge Hotel.

"Who would have known Buddy Bonz dog biscuits were this popular?" Gordo said.

"A chance at instant fame and ten thousand dollars in cash might have something to do with it," Lizzie told him. She looked around the lobby. "How will we ever find Baxter? There are dozens of golden retrievers here. They all look alike."

Miranda touched Lizzie's shoulder. "I agree, but don't ever let Vice Principal Putney hear you say that, okay. There's only *one* Baxter, remember?" Then she pointed to her watch. "And we have less than thirty minutes to find him and get him back to your house."

Gordo pointed to a magnetic easel. "Buddy Bonz spokes-dog auditions in the Rose Wing of the hotel."

Lizzie, Miranda, and Gordo rushed to the Rose Wing and started checking rooms. Most of the doors were closed.

"Should we knock?" Miranda asked.

"I guess so," Lizzie said. "We have no time to waste. And this *is* a total emergency."

"I sure hope the Buddy Bonz people think so," Gordo said.

"Shhh!" Lizzie put a finger to her lips. "I think I hear a very familiar voice coming from that suite."

With Gordo and Miranda right behind her,

she tiptoed to the door. Luckily, it wasn't locked. Lizzie turned the knob very quietly. Then she, Miranda, and Gordo slipped into the room.

It was dark, except for a spotlight on Matt, Lanny, and Baxter. They were standing on a small raised stage. A group of Buddy Bonz executives sat at a table across from them. They had their backs to Lizzie and her friends.

"Yes, sir, Baxter is my very own dog," Matt was saying. "I kind of share him with my best friend Lanny here." He put his arm around Lanny, who smiled and nodded.

"Tell us a little more about Baxter," a woman said. "Does he love Buddy Bonz treats? That's very important because our spokes-dog has to eat them by the truckload. It can take several hours and many takes to make just one commercial."

"Oh, sure," Matt said, with a wave. "They're his favorite."

Gordo slapped his hand to his forehead. "Can you believe this?" he whispered to Lizzie and

Miranda. "I've already established that Baxter hates Buddy Bonz."

"Maybe we should just run up there and grab him?" Miranda whispered.

A smile spread across Lizzie's face. "No, let's wait," she whispered back.

> I know we're running out of time. But this show is going to be too good to miss!

After bragging that Baxter couldn't live without his Buddy Bonz treats, Matt smiled at the casting directors, pulled a treat from the box, and held it up to the dog's nose.

Baxter didn't seem to care.

"Baxter, eat the treat!" Matt whispered. "Um, please?"

Baxter turned away and yawned.

The woman looked down at her clipboard. "I'm sorry, Mr., er, Carpenteropolis and friend, but Baxter is not the right dog for us. Thanks for coming and do pick up your free doggy-delicious treat bag on your way out. Next!"

"No, wait!" Matt said. "Did I mention that Baxter is a fully-pedigreed champion show dog? And he *loves* Buddy Bonz! He does. He can't get enough of them!"

Matt and Lanny started pulling more dog biscuits out of their enormous Buddy Bonz box, trying to get Baxter to eat them. But once again the dog yawned.

"Maybe he'd like one of these," Gordo said, stepping forward out of the darkness. He held up one of Baxter's bacon-flavored vitamin treats.

Matt shaded his eyes. "Uh-oh," he said to Lanny. "I think we may have hit another slight snag in our scheme."

"Gordo, where did you get that?" Lizzie asked.

Gordo shrugged. "I stuck a few in my pocket. I thought they might come in handy." He walked closer to Baxter with the treat.

When Baxter caught a whiff of his favorite treat, he lunged eagerly from his spot, knocking Gordo over. The treat went flying and so did Baxter. His large tail whipped through the room, knocking over cups of coffee, pitchers of water, videocassettes, and stacks of paper.

"Get that Buddy Bonz-hating animal out of here!" one of the casting people shouted.

"No problem, sir," Lizzie said. She grabbed Baxter with one hand and Matt with the other. "I have things totally under control."

Lizzie, Gordo, Miranda, Matt, Lanny, and Baxter all made it back to the McGuire house by six o'clock sharp, thanks to an emergency cell phone call to Mrs. McGuire's taxi service.

Vice Principal Putney's sister was just getting out of her car. "Baxter!" she cried when she saw the golden retriever. "Were you a good boy?"

"I think I'll just go and see whether the yard needs any cleaning up," Matt said quickly.

"Come on, Lanny, we have work to do."

After Ms. Putney left with Baxter, Lizzie faced her little brother and his perfect-penmanship pal. Miranda and Gordo stood with her.

"Okay," Lizzie snapped. "Spill."

"I can clear up this whole misunderstanding," Matt said. "Lanny and I just 'borrowed' Baxter for a couple of hours. We left a note so you wouldn't freak. Lanny even has a copy of it."

"A copy?" Lizzie said.

"He thought his first one was too messy," Matt explained. "So he did it over."

Lanny nodded and produced a crumpled piece of paper from his pocket. Lizzie took the note and smoothed it out. It read:

NO TIME TO SAY GOOD-BYE.
TOOK THE DOG (BAXTER) TO BONZ AUDITIONS.
HE'S GONNA BE A STAR
BUT KEEP THIS QUIET UNTIL WE GET THE CONTRACT!
BACK SOON,
M & L

"I admit, it's *possible* that I didn't latch the gate very securely in my hurry to get Baxter to the audition," Matt said. "Time is money, you know—Business Rule Numero Four. And I suppose it's also *possible* one of Ms. Harris's cats came by and the dogs chased it to her house."

Lizzie crossed her arms. "Any other *possibilities* I should know about, Dog Breath?"

"Hey, I didn't want you to worry," Matt said. "Honest. And I'm sorry all the other dogs got out. But the way I figured it, Vice Principal Putney would be really happy if Baxter became a big star. Maybe even happy enough to give you that Community Helper Award, and me and Lanny a *teensy* seventy-five percent agents' cut of Baxter's earnings. Oh, and by the way, you and I might *still* be able to work things out on this Doggy Day Care deal."

"Nothing to work out," Lizzie told her brother. "It's a *done* deal, and here's the 411: you and Lanny are *volunteering* to work for Doggy Day

Care every day for the entire spring break. Plus, FYI, I have a feeling you're going to be in the doghouse with Mom and Dad for a long, long time."

And good luck with Vice Principal Putney when *you* get to junior high!

T wo weeks later, Lizzie was hanging with Gordo and Miranda in her backyard again. Happily, on this particular Saturday, there were no dogs—or little brothers—in sight.

The three had returned to school this past week (after their *useful* and *rewarding* spring break) to find themselves the center of attention.

"I still can't believe we did it. Team Doggy Day Care actually won the Hillridge Community Helper Award," Miranda said shaking her head. "How incredible is that?"

"I couldn't have done it without you and Gordo," Lizzie said. "We're going to have a great time eating dinner at the mayor's mansion next month, and I'm glad you both agreed with me about the money."

"Yeah," said Gordo with a shrug. "That woman from the Hillridge Animal Shelter sure was happy."

The three friends had talked it over, and they'd all agreed to donate their thousand-dollar award, along with their Doggy Day Care earnings, to the needy shelter.

"I'm glad we did that," said Lizzie. "It was a great example. After they put our story on the local news, a lot more people decided to give money and volunteer at the shelter, too, including Mr. Barney and Ms. Harris. So, it really was worth it."

"Not to mention the look on Kate's face when the TV news crew showed up at school to interview *us*," Miranda couldn't help adding.

"Priceless," Lizzie agreed with a smile.

That wasn't even the end of it. The guys from the Audio-Visual Club finally got sick of Kate bossing them around, and, unlike Kate, they actually had consciences. So, when they got back to school after break, they'd turned Kate in for paying them to tear down all of Lizzie's Doggy Day Care posters. Vice Principal Putney was not amused. Now, Kate and her AV posse would be serving detention instead of *getting* served at the mayor's mansion.

is there a word to describe that special feeling when a person like Kate finally gets what's coming to her? Did i say *priceless*?

"Hey, there's someone I'd like you two to meet," Miranda told Lizzie and Gordo.

Lizzie and Gordo looked at each other. "Who?" Lizzie asked. "Is it a guy?"

"Not exactly," Miranda said. She reached down and lifted the flap on her big shoulder bag. Two sleepy little eyes peered out. "This is Scooter Two. We adopted him from the Hillridge Animal Shelter last night."

"Ooooh, he's so cute!" Lizzie cried.

"And so *small*," Gordo said. "Does he like Buddy Bonz biscuits?"

Miranda lifted the puppy out of her bag and gave him a kiss. "No weird experiments on *my* puppy!" she said.

Lizzie put an arm around her friend. "I'm officially retiring from the dog biz, Miranda," she noted. "But if *you* ever need doggy day care—"

"You can trust your pup to us!" Gordo said.

Want to have a way cool time? Here's a clue.... Read the next Lizzie McGuire Mystery!

# Case of the KATE HATERS

Cheerleader Kate Sanders, Lizzie's archrival, actually needs Lizzie's help. During a big pep rally, someone plays a prank that makes her look like a total laughingstock. Then members of the entire cheer squad start to become the victims of pranks that make them look bad, too. Is the guilty party one of Kate's enemies at school (too many to count!), someone a she-beast cheerleader dissed (too many to count!), or maybe it's that rival cheer squad from a nearby school.... Two, four, six, eight, supersleuth Lizzie's on the case!

**"A**nother tough case? Bring it on!**"**

a comedy of
psychic proportions!
that's so
raven
every day on
Disney Channel!
Disney
CHANNEL
Original
DISNEYCHANNEL.COM